P9-BUI-419

A Deans Tall Story Book

Puppy
Sam
Goes to School

A Deans Tall Story Book

Puppy
Sam
Goes to School

Illustrated by Douglas Hall

Puppy Sam had a brother
called Toby. Toby was old
enough to go to school.
In the mornings, Sam helped
Toby to get ready
for school.

Being at school looked
like lots of fun. Sam
didn't like going home
and leaving Toby
and all the laughter behind.

Being at home without Toby
was dull. Mummy was busy
doing housework. "I wish
I could go to school,"
thought Sam. Then
he had a naughty idea.
"I *will* go to school,"
he said to himself.

Sam hid by the front garden gate and watched for the postman to arrive, and then, oh dear, he slipped out through the open gate.

Sam ran along the road towards the school.
On the way, he saw a big bus and a motorcycle. When Sam got to the school, he ran into the playground.
He looked in through the classroom window and saw Toby reading to the teacher.
No one noticed Sam, which was lucky, as puppies are too young to go to school.
Sam was being naughty.

Just then the postman came
to deliver letters to the
school and *he* saw Sam.

"You should not be here,"
said the postman. "You are
a naughty pup. Come along,
I will take you home."
The postman took Sam by the
paw and took him home.

In the afternoon Sam and
Mummy went to meet Toby
from school. "I will not
tell Toby you have been
naughty," said Mummy to Sam.

"Toby likes to think that
you are always well-behaved."
  Sam was pleased.
"Good old Mummy!"
he thought.
So Toby never did know that
Sam had been to school and
Sam was never
naughty again — well,
not *very* naughty!

First published in 1985 by
Deans International Publishing
52–54 Southwark Street, London SE1 1UA
A division of The Hamlyn Publishing Group Limited
London · New York · Sydney · Toronto

Text and illustrations Copyright © Deans International Publishing,
a division of The Hamlyn Publishing Group Limited, 1985

ISBN 0 603 00422 9

All rights reserved. No part of this publication
may be reproduced, stored in a retrieval system,
or transmitted in any form or by any means,
electronic, mechanical, photocopying, recording or otherwise,
without the permission
of Deans International Publishing.

Filmset in Futura by Filmtype Services Limited,
Scarborough, North Yorkshire.

Printed and Bound by Purnell and Sons (Book Production) Ltd.,
Paulton,
Bristol.
Member of BPCC plc